Three Fools and a Horse

Three Fools and a Horse
by BETTY BAKER
Pictures by
GLEN ROUNDS

MACMILLAN PUBLISHING CO., INC.
NEW YORK
COLLIER MACMILLAN PUBLISHERS
LONDON

1 2 3 4 5 6 7 8 9 10

LIBRARY OF CONGRESS CATALOGING IN PUBLICATION DATA
Baker, Betty. Three fools and a horse. (Ready-to-read)
[1. Indians of North America—Fiction. 2. Apache Indians—Fiction] I. Rounds, Glen.
II. Title.   PZ7.B1693Th   [E]   75–14272   ISBN 0–02–708250–4

CONTENTS

1.
Little Fool

2.
Fat Fool

3.
Fool About

1.

LITTLE FOOL

A long time back,
the Foolish People
lived on Two Dog Mountain.
Most of the people
knew nothing.
Some knew
a little more.
But all of them
were foolish.

Three of them
went down the mountain.
They went to hunt buffalo.

Fool About said,
"A buffalo
is big and black.
If you see one,
tell me."

They came to the flat land.

"Here!" said Little Fool.

"Here is a buffalo!"

The others ran to him.

"It is big," said Little Fool.

"It is black," said Fat Fool.

"It is a bug," said Fool About.

"A buffalo
is the biggest thing
you ever saw."

They went far out
on the flat land.
"I see buffalo,"
said Little Fool.
"They are the biggest things
I ever saw."
The others ran to look.

"They are not black,"
said Fat Fool.
"They are not buffalo,"
said Fool About.
"Maybe they are
a new kind of dog."
"A new kind of deer,"
said Little Fool.
"Good to eat,"
said Fat Fool.

"Look!" said Fool About.
Some flat land men
came to the animals.

The men jumped up
and sat on the animals.

"Ah," said the Foolish People.
"If we could do that,
we would be big men,
the biggest men
of the Foolish People."
Fool About said,
"We must get one
of those animals."
"How?" said the others.
Fool About said,
"We will ask
one of those men
to race. Little Fool
will race with him."

The others laughed.

They all knew

that Little Fool

ran faster than anyone.

The flat land men
did not like
other people.
The Foolish People
knew that, too.

But they were too foolish

to be afraid.

They went to ask

a flat land man

to run a race.

A flat land man
with a big nose said,
"You do not have horses.
How can you race
without a horse?"
"What are horses?"
said Little Fool.

"This is a horse,"
said Big Nose.
"Ah," said the Foolish People.
The big animals were horses.
Fool About said,
"We do not need a horse."

The men from the flat land
laughed and laughed.
Big Nose said,
"Do you know how fast
a horse can run?"
"No," said Fool About.

"But Little Fool runs faster."
"Fast as the wind,"
said Fat Fool.
The men from the flat land
laughed harder.
"Let him race," they said.

Big Nose laughed, too.

It was not a nice laugh.

"Good, good," he said.

"If Little Fool wins,

he will get a horse.

If my horse wins,

I get Little Fool's nose."

"Cut off my nose?"

said Little Fool.

He liked his nose.

He wanted to keep it.

"Run! Run!"
called the Foolish People.
Little Fool ran faster
than ever before.

He ran fast,
fast as the wind.
The horse did not.
Little Fool won.

The Foolish People
were very happy.
They said, "Little Fool
is a big man!"

Big Nose wanted
to race again.
But the Foolish People
were not that foolish.

2.

FAT FOOL

Little Fool took his horse.
It looked as big
as Two Dog Mountain.
"Get on," said Big Nose.
Little Fool said,
"I do not need a horse.
I can run faster."

"I can't," said Fat Fool.

"But I can sit.

Push me up."

Fool About and Little Fool

got under him.

They pushed.

Fat Fool went over
the top of the horse.
All of the men
from the flat land laughed.

Fat Fool said,

"You pushed too much."

Little Fool said,

"I will get

on the other side.

Then you will not go over."

Fool About pushed

and Little Fool pulled.

The men from the flat land
laughed and laughed.
Fat Fool did not go over.
He sat on the horse.
But he was looking back.

He hit the horse
and said, "Turn around."
The horse walked away.
Fat Fool said, "Stop!"
and hit the horse.
The horse went faster.

"Stop the horse!"
said Fat Fool.
"I cannot see
where I am going!"
Big Nose laughed.
So did the others.

The Foolish People
ran to stop the horse.
Fool About pulled
the horse's tail.
It did not stop.

Little Fool ran
and pulled big sticks
in front of the horse.
The horse did not stop.
It went over the sticks.
Fat Fool fell off.

"Get the horse,"
said Fool About.
"Let it go," said Little Fool.
"We need it," said Fool About.
Fool About wanted
to go home on the horse.
He wanted to be a big man,
the biggest man
of the Foolish People.
Fat Fool said, "No one knows
how to stay on it."
"I know how," said Fool About.
"When we get up
on Two Dog Mountain,
I will show you."

Fool About took the horse
and they walked away.
The flat land men
were still laughing.

3.

FOOL ABOUT

The Foolish People
went up Two Dog Mountain.
Fool About said, "Stay here.
I must get something."
Fat Fool said,
"Get something to eat."
Fool About got a rabbit.
Then he walked away.

"It is just one rabbit,"
said Little Fool.
"A little rabbit,"
said Fat Fool.
Little Fool said,
"I wish it was a deer."
"Or a buffalo," said Fat Fool.

They wished and wished
but the little rabbit
stayed a rabbit.
Fat Fool said,
"A little rabbit
will make a big soup.
I will make soup."
Little Fool said,
"Do you know how?"
Fat Fool said,
"Anyone can make soup.
You put in this.
You put in that.
You let it cook
and then you eat it."

He put in this.

He put in that
and let it cook.

"Now eat," he said.

Little Fool said, "Is it good?"

Fat Fool said, "Eat it.

Then you will know."

Little Fool looked at it.
Then he said,
"Let the horse eat first."
They took the soup
to the horse.

The horse looked at the soup
and blew on it.
Then the horse walked away
and ate grass.
"The soup is bad,"
said Little Fool.
"The horse will not eat it."

So Little Fool and Fat Fool
would not eat the soup.

They went with the horse
and ate grass.

"I wish we had a deer,"
said Little Fool.

"I wish we had a buffalo,"
said Fat Fool.

Fool About came back.
He saw the soup
and ate it.

Then Fool About
went to the others.
He had sap
from pine trees.
He put the pine sap
on the horse.

He said, "Now I will stick
and not fall off."
And he did.
The horse ran and jumped
but Fool About
did not fall off.

He went home
on top of the horse.

The Foolish People said,
"Fool About is a big man."

Then Fat Fool said,
"Get down and eat."
"I ate," said Fool About.
Little Fool said,
"You did not sleep.
Get down."

But Fool About
could not get down.
Fat Fool and Little Fool
pushed and pulled.
But they could not get him
off the horse.

Little Fool took
the horse to the river.

All night and day
he washed
and washed.
At last he washed
the pine sap away.

Fool About got off the horse.

But he could not sit down
for many days,

and the Foolish People
laughed and laughed.

Author's Note

The Foolish People were a tribe the Apaches made up so they could tell jokes about them. But the jokes were more than funny stories. They taught important lessons to children: Don't run up to strangers, don't just sit around wishing for food, and so on. The best known are about the Foolish People and the horse, an animal the Apaches saw the Plains Indians riding. Many stories have been printed in folklore and anthropology magazines. They are often very short, some only a few sentences. Several have been combined, slightly changed and much elaborated in the writing of this book.